WE'RE. STILL. HERE.

WE'RE.
STILL.
HERE.

Published in the United States by FAST Press

Franklin, Tennessee

Library of Congress Control Number: 2025913819

ISBN Hardcover 979-8-9992051-0-0

ISBN Paperback 979-8-9992051-1-7

ISBN E-book 979-8-9992051-2-4

Cover Photo: Brett Jordan

Companion Title: *The Boy Who Came Up Fighting*

Book Template Courtesy of
https://williamson-tn.pressbooks.pub/

INTRODUCTION

I want to offer my sincere thanks to each member of my family; to every friend and teacher from whom I have received encouragement and some small nugget of insight or wisdom; to our literary heroes too numerous to mention, who walked with us through trying times. I would like to also thank the staff in the Special Collections department at Williamson County Public Library. They have been incredibly helpful.

The astute reader may recognize the boy who came up fighting as the muse and inspiration for this collection.

juan n der Wildnis

juan n der Wildnis

CONTENTS

CHAPTER 1

SUNDAY MORNING LEANING DOWN

I leaned across the pew,

Said "Nate, how are you?"

He looked at me so sad,

"Hi, Dad, I don't get to see you much."

He hugged my neck with such a tender touch.

Now my heart can never freeze or harden —

I felt the kiss of the Son in pardon.

May 11, 1975

juan n der Wildnis

CHAPTER 2

DAD'S ODE

Do not go gentle

Rang true in my easy chair

Beside the hospital bed

Assigned my dad.

Harsher sounds assault my mind.

Rage against the dying of the light

Epitomized

Legitimized

The fearless fight.

From down the hall a groan

Emphasized

The darkest curse of all.

Though you've never known

a villanelle,

nor written lies,

You gave me hope —

Fight like hell!

CHAPTER 3

STEPPING STONES

Through the thorny thicket

Into the brake of cane beside the sea

Faint of heart and weak of knee

I part the swaying reeds.

With flames hot on my heels

And smoke searing my lungs,

My peninsula shrinks,

Then shortly disappears.

How deep the stream?

How far the shore?

Way too far to swim,

As to peril, so unsure.

Not with courage, plan

Or determination

I turn at last and gaze

At the water, realize

If I take the plunge

At least I'll have a ticket

Out of this infernal circling blaze.

We jumped — I saw the sun

Dance upon the rippling surface

And the kid imagined

Butterflies were angels.

After thrashing madly in the depths

His little feet reached a solid

Rock, shallow enough to save

But too deep to easily find.

Was it planted just for us?

Had it served earlier as a millstone?

Was it part of an old road,

An earlier Via Dolorosa?

In any case, the stones appeared

At just the right time,

Time after time,

Lit by unseen lamp

For wandering feet.

juan n der Wildnis

CHAPTER 4

SOLD OUT

In the air, on land and sea —

No retreat, no surrender.

For tribute not a penny;

For truth and future,

Life itself.

In the hedges,

In the catacombs,

In the news or incognito —

Don't explain,

Don't complain.

In the streets,

In the prisons,

In the face of hopeless odds

Be of cheerful mien —

The world is much with us,

But not for long.

CHAPTER 5

DRAGGING THE NET

His first assignment after probationary training was to go online and rid that ethereal realm known as cyberspace of sexual predators, those despicable and lawless cowards who hide behind the anonymity of their computer screens and entice innocent, unsuspecting underage girls to abandon their families and, all too often, to meet an early death on an abandoned street corner or a rural road. Ricardo Miller had all the attributes the bureau was looking for in an agent: avid patriotism, instilled throughout his life by a grandfather who came to the U.S. from Mexico at the age of ten to pursue the American dream; military experience, in which he attained expert rating with both the M-16 and sidearms; a college degree in accounting, with an emphasis in forensic auditing; and, most importantly, a thorough familiarity with computer science, not merely as it related to games but also as that newfangled science lent itself to criminal misuse.

Agent Miller brought exceptional zeal to law enforcement, along with a moral rectitude that sometimes –that is to say, before new acquaintances got to know him better—grated on friends' nerves. His colleagues, and particularly the special agent in charge, regarded him as above temptation, committed to the impartial enforcement of the law of the land. Now it is true that Agent Miller was not included in most after-hour social events staged by his fellow agents, but that fact reflected favorably upon Miller, as Miller himself would have understood, because the tee-totaling R. Miller tended to look down on even the moderate consumption of alcohol or the occasional indulgence of a fine Cuban cigar that had somehow floated across ninety miles of open ocean (wink, wink.)

Now the special agent knew R. Miller's assignment, at least the thrust of his investigation. His officemates, however, had no inkling of Miller's objectives or, for that matter, his investigative technique. In that regard he turned to his own advantage a noticeable reticence. Some people, I have heard, if you ask them what time it is, they'll tell you how to put a watch together. Not Agent Ricardo Miller. Ask him what time it is and he's apt to say ten after. Initially his colleagues bristled at these incomplete answers, his refusal to volunteer information, but gradually and somewhat reluctantly the majority of them came to respect him even more, perceiving his personality to be that of a professional.

It was in the privacy of his own cubicle at the bureau that R. Miller devised his plan to identify and remove, one by one, the above referenced lowlifes that might target girls in cyberspace. So he was quite pleased with himself when he got the OK on his revised proposal of investigation. He would assume the identity of a minor, a girl of seventeen, enter a chat room and become friends with a man who showed interest in young girls. Then, after feeling him out, leading him on, and implying certain unspecified pleasures he, — or "she?" — would set up a meeting in a town near the John's home. Wham! Drop the hammer when the guy shows up!

Once he headed down this path R. Miller spared no effort in surfing the internet, looking for chatrooms and fora where predators might hide. After meeting and chatting with three or four prospective suckers he determined that he needed to lower his age. For one thing, in most states the penalty is much harsher for a man that dates a fourteen-year-old than for a man that dates a seventeen-year-old. Secondly, he surmised that the man who preys on younger girls would be more reckless, more out of control. Thus, he settled on his new identity. He would now be Barbra Olsen, cheerleader, crazy about boys, into music, and living in Los Angeles. Having observed the loose grammar, the shortcuts, the misspellings that the uneducated American public sprinkled through cyberspace, Agent Miller chose as his screen name "barBRA-in-LA."

Quite predictably barBRA began to get nibbles. R. Miller seethed at the realization that so many American men would brazenly seek out an underage girl and hope to actually set up a meeting. Nevertheless, he pushed ahead with his undercover work, painstakingly documenting names and pertinent data on the johns she — or he — talked to.

Within two weeks R. Miller was quite confident his work was about to pay off. A polite man of twenty-two, AZwolf, had ingratiated himself with barBRA, learned her interests, shared his own thoughts, and established a rapport. As barBRA gradually and somewhat cautiously allowed herself to become his friend the two exchanged addresses and feigned real care and concern for each other.

A week passed in which the two cyber friends chatted daily, and then Agent R. Miller got what he was looking for. Although he had refrained from suggesting a get-together, making sure he could defend his investigation against a charge of entrapment, he was thrilled when AZwolf informed her that he would be in Los Angeles next week, could they meet after school in some public place where she would feel comfortable, for after all, his feelings and thoughts were strictly for her own good.

Sure, barBRA told him, she was thrilled, would McDonald's be OK?

The appointed day came and barBRA could hardly wait, that is to say R. Miller could hardly contain himself. The prospect of nabbing an internet predator so early in his career; the ensuing publicity, mind you not for his benefit but to send a stern message to the scumbags, to make the world a safer place for law-abiding citizens; he caught a plane to LA and took a second agent with him as was the custom in the bureau, as well as an eighteen-year-old information tech from the office. She had quite good-naturedly dressed down to the level of a middle school student.

On the flight out Agent Miller explained for the first time the setup to his colleagues. The plan was simple: spot a twenty-two-year-old man, should be about 5'11," 180 pounds, dark hair, most likely would appear nervous, should walk in precisely at 4:30. And would be wearing a coat and tie since he is a successful businessman, in the import business, that's what was bringing him to LA. He reassured his little team that all was under control.

Miller's first doubt reared its ugly head when the threesome approached the designated McDonald's. barBRA and AZwolf had nailed down the time, the address, but there were two entrances. No problem he said to his partner, we'll split up and keep an eye on both doors as we sit with coffee and newspaper. barBRA would be forward and center. So the mandatory synchronization, the taking of position, the waiting, now 4:20. Customers came and went, not too busy, and Miller could feel the excitement build. The country needed this, the message needed to go forth, ...

There he was, sunglasses—sure, in disguise, probably married—walking in behind a rather plain-looking woman of thirty or so. The man, who might have passed for twenty-three or twenty-four glanced casually through the eatery and walked to the counter. Pretty calm, good actor, probably done this before, Miller thought to himself. Out of the corner of his eye he noticed the stocky, short-haired woman who came in with the suspect. Still looking around, she took a seat directly in front of barBRA without ordering. Then, after the man with sunglasses received his order he turned and headed toward the plain-looking woman's table. Did these two come in as a couple? No, he stopped short and took a seat ten feet from her and unwrapped his sandwich. He wasn't looking around, just focused on his meal, such as it was, R. Miller thought.

Agent Miller glanced at his watch. 4:30 on the money. As if on cue the woman rose, went toward the young tech's table and sat down. The suspect then approached the table of the two females. After Miller flashed the agreed-upon signal he walked up behind the suspect, service revolver drawn, and announced that the man in sunglasses was under arrest.

Maybe Miller shouldn't have actually touched the man's back with his service revolver. Maybe he should have approached him from the front. In any event, the suspect whirled in a flash, knocking Miller's right arm aside with his left arm, and firing three quick shots into Miller's neck with the 9 mm in his right hand. Miller's colleague immediately knocked the shooter's service revolver from his hand and placed him under arrest.

The newspapers and local television stations had a field day. How could one federal agent shoot another federal agent in broad daylight, in McDonald's of all places? In front of two innocent ladies, and with other upstanding citizens and fast-food workers all around?

Court testimony revealed that the murderer had followed the short-haired woman, a lesbian predator all the way from San Francisco, having secretly monitored her internet activity. He himself had been ready to effect her arrest when he felt a gun in the small of his back.

The shooter resigned from the bureau; the short-haired woman was remanded to the State of Arizona after her federal sentence of three years' probation was imposed; McDonald's ran a special on coffee for seniors; and the howls outside Tucson rose to more than mourning, even to grieving.

juan n der Wildnis

CHAPTER 6

THE HUNGRY ARTIST

It all began innocuously enough. Even as a toddler Frank H. had been slim, or as one might go so far as to say, gaunt. Mr. And Mrs. H. were heartened, however, not only by the child's hearty appetite, but also by the radiantly healthy glow of his cheeks. In spite of his conspicuous consumption, Frank H.'s parents could not "flesh him out."

Aside from his unusual dietary habits Frank H. led the rather typical life of a small-town youth, obedient to his parents, respectful toward his teachers, willing enough for church. Although he participated occasionally in youthful sports, he gradually became more and more withdrawn, not so much on account of shyness but more for the pure delight of "sketching and daubing," as he put it.

Frank H. was only vaguely aware that his circle of acquaintances knew him and referred to him in muffled snickers as Greedy Gut. This ridicule, which he told himself was good-natured in motive, he could easily put out of mind by immersing himself in his "sketching and daubing." So intense did his

21

artistic commitment gradually become that he began to see it as a quest for truth, a search for the ultimate essence.

The reason, in large part, for Frank H.'s widening fame was the relish and enthusiasm with which he attended church on the third Sunday in May. For generations his little church had celebrated that particular Sunday with an "All-Day Singing and Dinner on the Ground." By the time Frank H. reached the age of thirteen somebody had labeled it "All-Day Dinner and Singing on the Ground." Without doubt the worship was as sincere as ever, but to all outward appearances the young men of the congregation had turned the affair into an informal amateur eating contest.

Not only did Frank H. eat his opponents under the table, so to speak; he did it with a style, a flair that also became grist for the local gossip mill. Mannerly to others in the chow line; fastidious as he deftly applied the *serviette* to the corner of his mouth; prim with his right arm properly, almost casually, folded in his lap; deliberate and methodical in both the manipulation of his fork and his chewing; and seemingly unaware of a wide-eyed, open-mouthed audience, our subject presented a picture simultaneously deep and shallow, satisfying and upsetting.

At the risk of sounding commercial, Frank H.'s big break came shortly after his sixteenth birthday. As a fundraiser the Exchange Club was selling tickets for a Pancake Breakfast to be held some eighteen miles away in the county seat. The individual eating the most pancakes would walk away with $100.00 cash. As it happened Frank H. had longed for an art kit that would run about $90.00 or so, but that kind of price was far beyond his family's limited means. So, at the prodding of his mother in particular, Frank H. entered his first official, professional eating contest. To those in the audience on the appointed day who were more or less familiar with the legend of Frank H. the issue was really never in doubt. As a matter of fact, those in the know considered it a performance rather than a contest. No wonder, then, that the local newspaper reporter played down Frank H.'s victory and emphasized instead how he accomplished the feat. "Such good manners ... eats like a gentleman ... a real contrast to the fat slobs ... so confident and smug as to border on arrogance ... rising almost to the level of an art form." Unaffected by the philistine admiration, Frank H. had simply earned the money for the brushes, paints and supplies for which he had longed.

Equipped, finally, to express himself more fully, Frank H. underwent a virtual metamorphosis. As more and more local discussions turned to his victory he withdrew ever more deeply into his own private world, or hog-heaven as he noted disparagingly in his journal. By widening the gulf

23

between himself and his audience of begrudging admirers he made it even more difficult for them to understand him. How much had he ever earned for a picture? Why draw when you can pick up $100.00 for eating a passel of pancakes? Besides, Frank H. was undefeated and might get into the really big money!

From the beginning Frank H. had been oblivious to the fame and money others were now urging him to pursue. Alone in his cocoon, capturing the sun's rays, looking for the Mona Lisa of all snowscapes, dreaming of seeing Florence .... Still, he began to consider the advantages of the prize money.

For one thing, the local media had jumped on his story. When Frank H. decided to skip the Great Iowa Pig-Out, one wacky deejay had opined, "Frank H. will eat no rind before its time." And a newspaperman contributed, "Frank H. won't bring home the bacon." Although the attention smacked strongly of commercialism, Frank H. began to justify in his own mind the contests as a means to an end.

Another phenomenon, unheard of but true, beckoned our subject to taste the promised success. An *avant-garde* piano teacher had secretly saved Frank H.'s discarded and soiled napkins from the Third Sunday in May and from the Exchange Club's Pancake Breakfast. Having been enthralled by his methodology; by the flourish of his fork; by his regularity; and by his potential for greatness, she saw

24

modern art in the flecks and smudges on those trashed *servietten*. If she later proved deficient in her estimation of art maybe she could at least make a few bucks on such celebrity memorabilia in her booth at the weekend flea market. Imagine Frank H.'s surprise when he learned that Mrs. W., wife of a rather successful but not much admired provincial lawyer, had paid the piano teacher $100.00 for the odd and still meager collection.

More and more our hero began to realize that while he had made not one penny from his passion, a market of sorts had sprung up, a market of pop art where real money changed hands, the kind of money that might finance his Italian trip.... Never mind that trash instead of real art was the focus; never mind that his heart was not in the Mississippi Melon Marathon. With a little luck, if the cards fell right, he could retire from the tour, open a little salon ....

juan n der Wildnis

CHAPTER 7

PRIMORDIAL OOZE

Once primordial ooze

Squeezed between the toes

Of a prehistoric Oz.

Then a poet whose

Breathy specious ooh's

Signified to us the blues —

His enraptured ah's

Camouflaged the blahs

In a hero's last hurrahs.

Now the setting sun

Motivates or prods

Hardly anyone

To attempt the talk of gods,

Neither flow'ring rose,

Snowy peak on high,

Wintry wind that blows,

Lemmings as they die.

Leave behind the slime,

Poet in his prime,

Maudlin epitaph in rhyme.

Couple truth with love —

Doubly precious cornerstone.

Then if push should come to shove

You will not be heard to moan.

CHAPTER 8

ART'S PLACE

In Burr County one can always quench the worst thirst and usually procure safe food in a number of roadside establishments. Several of these joints have built for themselves, along with a substantial customer base, somewhat unsavory reputations. Up until two years ago I frequented Art's Place almost exclusively. But Easter weekend saw some peculiar and disturbing developments, the official explanation of which raised more questions than it answered.

Before I recount those developments, even before I tell you about the clientele at Art's Place, I really should introduce you to Art. Only in knowing him will you be able to appreciate the diversity and genius of his customers. You yourself know that the personality of one individual, namely the proprietor, often shapes the flavor, the nuances, the conversations, the sounds, the fragrances exuded in a country beer joint. I say country, but in reality, Art's Place straddled the line demarking incorporation for the town of Palestine, i.e. the "city limits" cut Art's Place in two. There was a simple

29

reason for this so-called coincidence. When Art was initially seized of the entrepreneurial spirit, albeit feebly, he had vacillated between a rural business and an urban business. Admittedly, the incorporation of a town in Jackson County hardly renders the town's inhabitants or their collective enterprises "urban," but contrasted to the unchurched and uneducated folk on the rural routes, Palestine was a metropolitan haven for cosmopolitan mavens.

Art's vacillation between rural and city resulted in the construction of his place of business directly on the city limit line. By confining his beer sales to the western portion of the building, and doing paperwork and grilling in the eastern section, Art was able to comply with the city ordinance against selling beer within the city. Evidently his decision proved fortuitous, for both the rural yahoos and the city dwellers heartily supported his endeavor, judging from the packed parking lot and frequent deliveries by eighteen-wheelers.

Now Art had eschewed professional consultation in his site selection. Neither of the county's realtors would have approved the hillside spaghetti farm he eventually settled on. The parking lot consisted mainly of a long gravel strip that allowed customers to park their pickups, cars and logging trucks side by side, front tires arrested in their northward progress by a series of discarded crossties. Art had thus shrewdly limited his liability by positioning these

30

cross-ties in such a way as to discourage his customers from pulling too far off Highway 70 and plunging down the precipice that had made the site so affordable in the first place.

I have already mentioned Art's vacillation during the site selection and start-up. I suppose that is to be expected when one mind is home to two views. In Art's case, his business savvy and desire for independence were counter-balanced with a solid liberal arts training he had picked up down at State University. So, even though he knew how to reconcile his checkbook and figure his own taxes, he prided himself on his ability to connect with his customers, professional and blue-collar alike, on topics as diverse as politics and history, the price of persimmon wood for golf club heads, courthouse shenanigans, to name but a few. It goes without saying that he was particularly at ease while holding forth on country music and religion, yet never missing a beat while drawing a glass, popping tops or making change.

But regarding that Easter weekend — Bubba Yarboro and Joe Bob Dixon were holding down a couple of barstools when this fellow (Mason was his name they learned later) strolled in and ordered a Schaefer, draft please, and turned to the big screen TV after duly noting that not a single female was in the joint. Right away Bubba and Joe Bob pegged this new customer as a New Yorker, maybe a Jerseyite. And when Mason let fly with a string of expletives in response to a TV message about an upcoming Easter celebration, the two of them looked at each other in disbelief. Sure, we might all have our little faults, but nobody in his right mind would question the resurrection of the Good Lord. And only an utterly lost soul would cuss on such a religious topic.

Now contrary to the stereotypes bandied about by visitors and foreigners, every little dispute in Burr County was not and is not settled by brass knucks, knives, etc. Thanks in large part to their mothers, who had passed down a thread of morality, or at least a filament of civility, Bubba and Joe Bob retired to the little add-on back room for a dart match. They themselves weren't active in church and civic affairs, but they were good people, i.e. they came from good families and they both had some degree of motivation to steer clear of trouble. Bubba had inherited an inordinate fondness for homebrew, and that batch tainted with rat poison had hardly sharpened his judgment. If ever a man needed the restraint and counsel of a trusted friend, it was Bubba.

Joe Bob was that friend, and Joe Bob did his best to keep Bubba calm. Instrumental in that effort was keeping Bubba from consuming too much alcohol too fast. He remembered enough chemistry from high school and one semester at State, seasoned with observation, to know Bubba's limit in a given time period, taking into account his friend's considerable body weight. On top of his formal education, Joe

Bob had practical know-how that would have surprised his mom and dad had they known about his experiments with that chemistry set they gave him for his fourteenth birthday.

So now Joe Bob's motivation to avoid trouble was twofold. His probation officer was keeping a close watch on him, and his own brother was District Attorney. Both had given him to understand that one more scrape with the law would send him up the river. They wouldn't be able to sweep it under the rug again, or as the probation officer phrased it, "look the other way." Besides, the DA was building himself a nice political career by fulminating against and prosecuting the use of illegal drugs.

So these two boys weren't looking for trouble. Far from it. Even though Mason's blasphemous tirade had momentarily taken them aback, they had put the incident behind them and were raucously enjoying their dart match and cold brews. That was when Mason came through the dart room, intending to relieve himself from the back stoop, seeing as how the men's room was occupied. But all hell broke loose before he enjoyed that relief. As this out-of-towner strolled between the dartboard and the contestants (some later alleged that he "swaggered" through, while one said he "lollygagged" in front of Joe Bob and Bubba) Bubba's dart nailed Mason in the temple. I suppose it was the body's involuntary reaction or some such, but Mason clutched his head, emitted a panther-like blood-curdling scream and lunged forward through the flimsy back door and sailed head over heels down that same precipice that rendered the property useless to all save Art. Naturally the scream and the racket of splintering plywood drew Art and the handful of local stalwarts into the dart room. There Bubba was explaining, "It was a accident. I didn't mean no harm. For Chrissakes ... he walked right in front of me."

One of the younger customers opined, "Shouldn't we try and go down the hill after that feller?"

But Bubba and Joe Bob were already anticipating repercussions, being somewhat acquainted with investigative techniques, and were loath to handle Mr. Mason and thus possibly open themselves up to even more suspicion than their innocent accident had already aroused. Yes, it was their accident, not Bubba's, even though it was Bubba's dart that did the damage. Nobody else had seen the culprit, not even poor Mason, except for Joe Bob. And as much as the two friends had been through and faced together, two things were certain: neither would confess to anything, and neither would rat on the other.

Art, of course, in spite of his business acumen and knack for management was hardly prepared for an emergency in which a customer's well-being, perhaps his life, was at stake. As owner he had sole responsibility not only for the arty décor, consisting mainly of graffiti and bumper stickers plastered on the walls and ceiling, but a responsibility as well to notify the authorities in the event of injuries on the premises. As he understood it, however, there were limits on his liability, and he half-consciously recalled a couple of phrases, perhaps from an Oscar-winning actor, along the lines of "what would a prudent and reasonable man do" and "exercising due diligence."

As the little crowd peered out the shattered door, beyond where the ramshackled back stoop and two-by-four railing had been, one last high-pitched horrific shriek pierced the darkness, and the thrashing in the underbrush subsided. As of one mind the cluster of drinking buddies fell silent. For the first time they had all grasped the possibility that Mason could actually be dead. Eventually the youthful customer, the one who had initially suggested going to Mason's aid, asked, "Reckon we ought to call the Sheriff?"

No sooner did the word "Sheriff" leave the guy's lips than three or four simultaneously correct him, pointing out that the chief of police had jurisdiction. After all, Art's Place was in the city.

"Hold on a minute," interrupted Art, who was intimately familiar with local ordinances, jurisdictions and city limits. "Part of this building is in the city, but the western part is outside the city limits. In fact the line runs through the dart room, and since Mason was not inside the the city when he got hit, maybe we should indeed call the Sheriff, who has county jurisdiction.

"But aren't you overlooking the fact," asked still another, "that whoever threw that dart was standing in the east end of the room, and if there's been a crime — I repeat, if — then the Chief of Police should be involved.

"Good point," joined in Joe Bob, who saw himself benefiting from the confusion and uncertainty permeating this amateur legal analysis. He knew that if charges were to be brought — either by the Sheriff or by the Chief — it would be his own brother, the DA, serving as prosecutor. But the longer that name didn't come up the better it suited Joe Bob. So, perhaps to muddy the waters further and to keep the discussion off the DA, Joe Bob raised a germane issue.

"Wouldn't the location of Mason's body — Mason, I mean — have a bearing on who has jurisdiction? I mean, where is he? In town or outside of town?"

Nobody knew Mason's exact location, let alone his condition. The gathering finally agreed to call the Sheriff, basing its decision on an argument advanced by none other than Bubba, who volunteered, "The city is in the county but the county ain't in the city."

Art was to reflect back on this pithy insight, and the pickled rube from whom it bubbled, as a rare and original diamond in the rough as he liked to tell himself. Bubba's intent, however, had perhaps less to do with set theory and more to do with his recollection of how much better the food was at the county jail than the slop they had thrown at him in town.

In about twenty minutes the Sheriff and two deputies arrived. The low and respectful voices fell silent when the officers finally completed the ascent and awkwardly but gently laid Mason's body in their hand-me-down-from-the-Feds combination rescue vehicle/ambulance. The Sheriff directed one of his deputies to cordon off the dart room and the entire precipice, and then gruffly ordered the crowd to stay away from the scene. Not too surprisingly the crowd drifted away and Art closed early.

Some say the wheels of justice grind slow but they grind fine. That depends on the meaning you attach to fine, for one thing. And here's another — those wheels can grind fast in a southern hamlet when the victim is a New Yorker or New Jerseyite. And if the DA is a brother to one of the suspects the wheels are greased and turbocharged. In this case a cursory preliminary investigation revealed that the two witnesses had remained mum, and were thus of no help to the public servants. In addition, there were legal questions at issue concerning jurisdiction, where did the accident or injury occur, where did the body come to rest, and did Mason die from the dart or from that headlong tumble down that deadly precipice?

Word also began to leak out that the discussion that Mason had joined at the bar was more heated than initially thought. On top of his profanity regarding the Resurrection, Mason made lowlife obscene comments about the Master's mother, and some of the patrons admired Joe Bob and Bubba for walking away from trouble. Two or three letters to the editor revealed a sentiment in the community, almost an attitude of resentment that Mason had picked this little town and Art's Place to have his unfortunate accident. The DA privately wondered if he could find twelve impartial jurors. In due course, and after requisite consideration, the chief prosecutor reluctantly concluded that the actions of the two suspects in the inquiry re the decedent Mason did not rise to the level of probable cause, and the case would be retired without prejudice.

By the Monday morning after the case was dropped, a note from the County Health Department was stapled to the front door of Art's Place: Closed by Order of the Health Department. Being both educated and experienced Art knew that when it comes to taking care of business the Court House Gang knows how to do it. So, while the suspects went about their lives; their lawyers swapped cars and went about their lives and affairs; the DA's popularity soared; and the newspaper's circulation increased, Art's Place was unceremoniously and without official explanation shut down.

If all the world's a stage, then each of these characters had a role to play. But there's no place for Art.

juan n der Wildnis

CHAPTER 9

REBEL YELL

Hear the rebel yell,

blood-curdling defiant

bone-chilling in the mad charge

oblivious to the cannon balls

courting death for a lost cause

lief to grapple man to man

get there fustest with the mostest

body parts tissue blood

including gutsbrainshairexcrement

Fightin' Joe Wheeler

Shiloh Gettysburg Chickamauga

other affectionate buzzwords

meant to raise the hair

on a red neck

Now the demon wail

subsides and countless rows

of crude markers denote

the supposed remains

of half-starved out-gunned out-numbered

heroes.

Rivers of blood gangrene malaria

twenty percent of Mississippi's

post-war budgets for artificial limbs

post-traumatic stress nightmares

suicides shot from behind throats cut

but service required for candidates

to be elected

Debate the right of one man or one class

to own another

do unto others

as you would have them ....

Since Appomattox

things haven't been black and white.

June 3, 1999

juan n der Wildnis

CHAPTER 10

ANOTHER IRAQI CASUALTY

Angry?

Me, angry?

Whatever gave you that idea?

Seeing me with no arms?

And one leg?

Nah — I hardly miss those accessories.

Sie wurden mit meinem einzigen Sohn begraben.

May 13, 2007

juan n der Wildnis

CHAPTER 11

LADY LANGUAGE

Language,

stolen by impostors,

perverted, even prostituted

in proverbial disregard

for truth —

your edge is my beginning.

Conception came before,

when words were hard to utter.

Even action reared its head

before the thought was said.

Language, since you came

I hardly know my name,

but I know that thought and deed

and truth

will never be constrained

to fit a pigeonhole.

The shattered stone and splattered bone

guaranteed the need for fleshly word

of truth.

Lady language, you were third,

secondary, necessary,

substituting ease of eyes and ears

for use of mind and soul.

Even so, the message on your back

was welcomed as redeeming

truth.

Language, your demise is my beginning.

You will be already long since gone

when I am fully grown,

when I am fully known.

Judge/disparage not this flimsy ship
when you hear this common quip:
"Silence is golden."

juan n der Wildnis

CHAPTER 12

MUSCADINE ROW

I know

my muscadine row

like a Good Book.

Thumbed and leafed through,

always yielding anew,

it often hides the ripest fruit

from casual eyes.

Though it satisfies

in season,

its punch improves with age.

And my muscadine row

enriches its environs,

even as it gives new life

to those who dig.

The leaves begin to turn —

speckled, spotted, stained.

With the quiet fall

of each leaf

the yield intensifies,

until at last I'm left

with the vine

and all it implies.

CHAPTER 13

STALIN

The man of steel

bolted a fragmented union together

with tanks, bullets and spikes.

Liquidation and the threat thereof

combined with forced labor

were the glue and the seal

eagerly supplied by the likes

of Beria, Zhukov and Khruschev.

Ferrous Felix

reminds me of

our own Eddie Aitch —

you give me the belly ache

with your paid informing agent

behind every mailbox.

Check the Iron Icon

toppled at last by unity.

Goodbye to your pressing image;

hello to sovereign Uzbekistan.

Now the Baltics have

bolted the fragmented union together.

April 23, 2003

CHAPTER 14

HOLLMAN ON LOOKING INTO HEANEY

Though our leaders shame us

(including chicken-dick Cheney)

as do also Blair and Thatcher

we insist on courage —

rather one should die with barley seeds apocket

than in a gated nursing home with

Halliburton oil oozing down his leg.

Here a poem that resonates,

there an ode that gives the spine a shiver,

the eye a tear,

the soul a jolt

of otherworldly hope.

The troubles have resumed;

peace again is doomed.

Come spring we'll see a shoot

of barley 'mongst the daffodils

and wonder whether some poor devil

gave his all defending hearth and gate.

Or springs the sprout

In face of doubt

To validate

Global agribusiness

As his slayer

Used to promulgate?

From this island

let the word

at last be heard:

we are biding

time, my friend;

and all the guilty gilded gates of hell

shall not prevail against that word.

juan n der Wildnis

CHAPTER 15

DAD'S LAMENTATION

What do I care for my soul

if my boy be gone to the fire?

What do I care for my body

if my girl be gone for good?

Let me deliver my boy

from the flame, from the coal;

let me retrieve my girl

from the pit of lost love.

Then when I descend

through death's dizzying whirl

I shall lay my soul, my body, my all

at I AM'S feet for a good while.

juan n der Wildnis

CHAPTER 16

3X5/ MAJESTIC SETTING

3×5

Make a note —

If you vote

Pick the man.

Parties plan,

Rule by rote.

MAJESTIC SETTING

Blazing through a purple hue

It ends its western trek.

Tinged with pink it

Frames the clouds from underneath

And gives the moon —

Descendent as it were —

A face of warmth.

Nov. 1991

CHAPTER 17

EYES ON THE PRIZE

3:13

9/16

22

years ago.

Can it be?

Did you know

I would go

To the very gates of hell

For the friend that sticketh closer

Than a brother?

And that's saying a Lot.

2005

juan n der Wildnis

CHAPTER 18

GROWING CORN

It won't amount

to a hill of beans

if you try to grow rich.

Prepare the field well;

else the seed is stolen,

rots or never takes root.

Plant the kernels at the right depth,

at the proper distance.

Time is a must

in growing corn.

It can't be forced,

it must be born.

Pray for rain,

pull the weeds,

pick the bugs,

pray again.

Watch it grow

of its own accord,

as it were.

It is its own reward.

Save enough seed

for next year's crop

before you hone the blade

and begin to chop.

Then at last

to store it right

fill it fast

and pack it tight.

CHAPTER 19

PANAMA JACK

Panamaniac,

blitz us once again

with denials,

obfuscations.

You, too,

take the tack of Ike

and act like Jack

when the Castro fiasco

                        back-

fired.

Tricky Dick

could imagine no

line so fine:

"I'm not a crook."

And Ronnie Rambo,

having bravely liberated Granada,

couldn't even hear the questions.

Say it ain't so, Eli. Hey!

You ran the CIA;

you know history.

Why lie?

CHAPTER 20

KRISTEN'S THEME

Purple hull peas,

Purple hull peas,

Pass them, please,

Purple hull peas.

Purple hull peas,

Purple hull peas,

Pass those peas,

Purple hull peas.

Purple hull peas,

Purple hull peas,

I'm down on my knees,

Begging you, please,

Pass those peas,

Pass them, please,

Purple hull peas.

July, 1999

CHAPTER 21

ABSOLUTION

poetic arse,

deal in sparse

imagethoughtfarce

dream the sublime

forgetting forced rhyme

go with gorsed thyme

ablaze in brassen thurible

aroma ascending Parnassus

wordlessly

but with its own angelic tongue

rising swirlingly

in a cathartic

and wholehearted

absolution

Feb. 16, 1999

ROAS'N'EAR ROWS

Roas'n'ear rows

roas'n'ear rows

look at those rows

hoe those rows

each one grows

bends and bows

look at those rows

roas'n'ear rows

Corn on the cob

yessirree, Bob

heck of a job

ravens will rob

pickin' a gob

corn on the cob

yessirree, Bob

corn on the cob

SHALOM

Shalom, sabon,

And get thee gone

Out of birthing Zion.

So long, Haiphong;

Was Fonda wrong,

Or was Lyndon lying?

Tze Tung, Mekong,

And My Lai song —

Are the orphans crying?

Roll on caisson.

Deposit one,

Noble clan's own scion.

From south to north

The tanks go forth

In the name of peace,

And west to east

They suffer least

Who refuse to cease

Producing arms,

Inflicting harms.

So the weak are dying.

If war is hell

Then toll the bell —

Millions more are dying.

May 1998

CHAPTER 24

THE MOON

Silvery sliver

and flaxen wafer

you wax and wane

blowing hot and cold

revealed in part

concealed in part

generating neither

heat nor light

as you march across

the starry ether

a loner as you arc

your lunar course

in a vain display of bright

yellows ambers gold

but carefully you hide

that darker side.

1999

CHAPTER 25

THE VALLEY STILL

The valley still

Neither frond nor leaf

Waves its neighbor "hi."

E'en the frailest flower

Is frozen to the eye.

O, death is nigh

If not the grief.

Where the power

When all about is still?

Spores to transport —

Spreading pheasant wings to prove —

Feathery fleets to bear aloft

O'er the ramparts of fancy's fort ....

Breathe again, my Zephyr friend,

Breathe upon me ever soft.

Intercede in this the hour;

Hear my groans and move.

CHAPTER 26

A REAL GOOD WAY

A real good way

to start the day.

And may I say

I drove on onion skins

with water splashing on my feet

without the benefit of wipers

afraid to fill the tank

a slipping transmission

and Christmas gifts a distant memory.

But I knew whom

I had believed

and was persuaded

that He was able.

Let the redeemed say so.

Well, it's all icing on the cake

when you've seen prayers answered,

experienced hope replacing despair,

discovered peace when your faith

trumped any agonizing doubts.

Hopeless of grace

yet I clung to the hope of grace.

I've seen it now and then,

and I have a witness,

how One can speak it into being.

CHAPTER 27

LARGE AS A BARGE

Large as a barge and in charge —

And "I paid for that mike."

Besides, Susan Smith wouldn't have

Drove her boys in that lake

If it hadn't been for those liberal policies.

Which reminds me ...

We wouldn't have had all these problems

Over the years if the whole country

Had voted for Strom.

May I mention, too,

That somebody has to be in charge.

I have not claimed to be in charge

Of much, but you ain't driving my boy in the lake.

And you ain't nigh as large as you talk.

True, you can measure a man in different ways,

And I freely confess I have fallen short,

But today the word goes out:

I am in charge of telling you,

"You ain't in charge."

May 9, 2004

CHAPTER 28

NICKIE'S BIRTHDAY

for Mar.27, 1999

It's your special day.

What can I say?

You're turning twenty-nine

and still looking so fine.

It's not just grandpappy

that you make happy.

Everybody you meet

knows just how sweet

you have been all your life

as a daughter, mother, wife.

As you get close to thirty

you're just as purty

as you ever were.

You would make me purr

if I were a cat

and I'd fly by night

if I were a bat.

You are a precious sight

and we love you so —

maybe more than you know!!

It's hard to measure

spiritual treasure

but it's extra nice

to know a pearl of great price.

And though we sometimes bug her

we still want to hug her.

She gets mad when we tease her

but she forgives granddad, the old geezer.

Since that day in nineteen seventy

knowing her has been heavenly.

To one of the world's great mothers:

keep on blessing others!!

Mar. 26, 1999

juan n der Wildnis

CHAPTER 29

20 MILLION

Sickle-symboled state —

monolithic emblem

or amalgam of variety?

Separated by tongues;

united by fanatic love

of a ravaged holy motherland;

home to hurt and grave to hope;

cruel secrets aired in open danger.

Beria, Sakharov and Brodsky,

Kerensky, Lenin, Trotsky —

a tendril here for war,

antenna there for peace.

Buffered by reluctant friends

in remembrance of the French,

the Nazis on the march,

she suffers on the snowy steppes

and stations cosmonauts in space.

Twenty million — what a price —

and most a wasted sacrifice

to the idol at the top.

Oct. 1988

CHAPTER 30

FRAGMENTS AND SCATTERTHOUGHTS

A lovely poem

read on Father's Day,

an attempt to capture love

between a father and his son.

Handwritten, he took it home,

lost it, now I can't recall the lines.

No rosetta stone to help me reconstruct

my nod to him and Enkel, Keats as well.

Kindred spirits, you and I,

been that way a long long time.

- - - - - - - - -

Didn't have to drive to Arkansas.

Kindred spirits, you and Keats,

- - - - - - - -

Beauty or truth, either beats the law.

CHAPTER 31

SCRUTINIZED

quarks velocity

inverse attraction

reciprocity

equal and opposite reaction

string them all together

and figure whether

one might see halley's comet twice

but if it all should end in ice

before that orb comes 'round again

tell me why a man and wife

who hoped for half a life

made of molecules

but free of pustules

should know pain

from the start

and tell me why the human heart

insists on hoping

even as it is groping

to reduce the universe

to the irreducible

in a confounded crucible

what's worse

hopeless of grace

yet clinging to the hope of grace

or arrogance

in elucidating chance

and every circumstance

and falling on your face

Apr. 26, 1999

CHAPTER 32

THE PROMISE KEEPER

Whose goods these are I think I know.

The silver in this world below,

the cattle on a thousand hills,

the gold beneath Alaskan snow —

they all belong to Him who fills

the mountain streams and woodland rills,

the rural ponds and inland seas,

with spotted trout and sweet bluegills.

The wealth of nations, if you please,

Is His alone to spend or freeze,

invest or waste on one lost sheep,

or pitch into the summer breeze.

This truth is lovely, constant, deep.

And He has promises to keep ...

to be fulfilled before I sleep,

to be fulfilled before I sleep.

Nov. 4, 1997

CHAPTER 33

TRUTH AND FICTION

It's no dereliction

of duty to opt for fiction

when fumbling and groping for the truth.

The ten virgins —

men swallowed by sturgeons —

"Whither thou goest" by Ruth —

Maybe he had a reason

other than teasin'

and sheltering the youth.

For example, sir,

it may be a blur

but you've made mistakes.

Shall we tell the simple facts

about your criminal acts

or count you among the fakes?

Or should we embellish

your laughably hellish

stab at goodness,

and call saintly

deeds that strongly

resemble rudeness?

The beauty of His

loving approach is

I don't have to fudge

or settle a grudge

in thinking of you.

His mercy is such

that he who was forgiven much

loves more than the man

who sticks to his own plan

in deciding what to do.

Making you small

Won't help me at all,

And sanctifying

a covetous lying

sonofabitch

who could make me rich

would help me even less.

So, by the process

of elimination —

to the world's consternation —

a gripping story

of earth-stopping glory,

constant, invariable

comes in forma parable.

March 1999

juan n der Wildnis

CHAPTER 34

ODE TO WILLIE

A dozen years pass,

and we're "taking oil and kicking ass."

My neighbor on the right

Takes my kid and robs me blind

So, I attack the one on the left

Since the first one's hard to find —

Guess he's hiding in the rock that's cleft.

Yeah, we heard from brain-damaged Bush

And lard-ass dope-head Rush.

Along with buck-nekked Dr. Laura

And the morals czar Bennett

They're all shredding the aura

That their mantra has worth in it.

Space will hardly permit

A recitation of all the shit

This gang has broadcast,

Nor the patriotic veterans

Who in truth were better ones

Than the fag-bashing flag-waving

Draft-dodgers whose non-military past

Seems to spawn a tax-cut craving.

Leave it to a redheaded stranger

To point out the danger

Foisted on us by a power-hungry clique,

Wherein the puppet controlled by Dick

Is like unto his predecessor

Except this one's confessor

Must account for horrendous loss of life

Instead of sins against one's wife.

Sing it loud, Willie, sing it true,

For we already know the dirt on you.

They can't tell us anything new.

We expect the malice

Of a fair and balanced

Network to be trained on your song.

We expect the Wills and the Novaks

To prove again that effete hacks

Were never right but always wrong.

Cannot be right, can only be wrong.

Jan. 2, 2004

juan n der Wildnis

CHAPTER 35

PERKS OF POWER

Did the jerk

With the smirk

Really shirk

His National Guard work?

Doth there lurk

Behind FERC

A Mr. Burke

Who tried to bribe the Turk?

Sometimes a quirk,

Like, say, Dunkirk

Vaults a Church-

Hill above the murk.

But oft the jerk

Will exert

A world of hurt.

Feb. 12, 2004

CHAPTER 36

SUNSET/ READ HIS LIPS/ MUSE

SUNSET

Reflected beams-

Refracted rays-

Cascading light-

Echoes through an empty vault.

1991

READ HIS LIPS

He claimed to be a words-

mith

But from his early youth

He couldn't tell the truth

Couching obfuscations rather

In circumlocutionary blather.

Here's a Handi Wipe, forsooth,

To clean up his words-

with.

1991

MUSE

Muse, how muffled your padded gait.

Was the quietness of your exit

courtesy or escape?

I had just begun to know you.

Have you spent your ninth life at last?

Calico chameleon, metamorphosing

evanescent ambiguity-

since I can't grasp

you lay hold of me

gently

with your clawing clasp.

1991

CHAPTER 37

THE LEADING LAWYER

To the leading lawyer's lair

Tramped a lady of the night.

There she poured repentant tears

On a stranger's dusty feet,

Kissed them, dried them with her hair —

Even wasted dear perfume

To the consternation of

Simon. Oh, cathartic moan —

Empty alabaster urn —

Outward signs of heartfelt love

Lost on pharisaic minds.

Shall it be until the Man

Works his perfect will on earth?

'Til the meek adore the Word,

That redemptive second birth?

"Meister, sprich!"

CHAPTER 38

NUMB AND NUMBER

7/20/2020

One, two, snatch that shoe.

Three, four, close the door.

Five, six, pick up sticks.

No, more like Thesis 96

or Avagadro's number.

Or a number that sticks in your mind like 6,

or 28, both perfect.

But 7 reminds some of heaven.

Numb yet?

10,000 dead from Covid-19, 20,000 projected.

A week later you hear of more.

Now they report 5,000 recovered.

I don't recall LBJ or Uncle Walter

telling us that 200,000 weren't killed last week,

or that 2,600 suffered a scrape last week

but have now recovered.

You really think we'll hit 50,000 deaths in 2 months?

But, on the bright side, a vaccine is on the way.

Wait, what will the anti-vaxers say about that?

Meanwhile, the number who have recovered,

despite the shortage of PPE and ventilators,

has skyrocketed to 18,000!

Expect a 100,000 dead? It's a hoax, a deep-state lie.

Some people say drink Clorox,

or drink aquarium cleaner,

and the virus will magically disappear

when the hot weather gets here.

And, thank goodness, children and infants need
have no fear.

Do numbers count?

Yes, watch the president's numbers mount —

$400,000 from his campaign donations

to his personal businesses in 2 days.

How is he wrecking our lives?

Let me count the ways.

Numb and Number

9/25/2020

Still They Slumber

So, Count No 'Count

descends from the mount

and massages, nay distorts,

his debts, his wealth, the truth,

even the deaths of everyone who supports

his psychotic pronouncements.

For the umpteenth time —

more like 20,000 by actual count —

he validates the maxim,

figures don't lie

but liars can figure. Now, 6 to 9 months in

113

we have recorded not a decline

from 15 to 0

but an explosion of dead souls

to the tune of 204,000, on top of

bursting hearts, corroded karotids

and organ failure.

One Caesar after the other;

Louis, Louis, all the way to 16;

one too many Henry's it would seem;

and the same for Mad King George.

Now we hear rumblings of successors

to Donnie Little-dick, like Don Jr.,

Ivanka, Eric, and why not Barron?

That has a certain ring to it, don't you think?

I'm thinking along the line of 10 to 20 for Barr,

20 to 30 for Stone, no parole.

Throw in life for the illegitimate president,

3 to five for Bolton (hold the razor),

and for as long as it takes, put Stephen Miller

into the company of blacks and Mexicans

(I've heard they're a bunch of rapists)

and wake me from the nightmare when you hear

that one or more succumbed to his/her fear

and played the MacFarlane part of craven coward,

dodged the pen and overdosed.

Numb and Number

12/13/2020

Knock, Knock, Knock,

Knocking three times on the devil's door.

10,000 and then 25,000 —

from 50,000 to a 100,000 —

and then 200,000 more —

now almost 300,000

precious lives sacrificed

to the dear leader who enticed

the troubled and the gullible.

Together they reduced to rubble

the norms, the rules of the road,

of a historic noble experiment.

All the while cheating

on families, taxes and wives

and arrogantly treating

others like chess pieces,

or cogs in production equipment.

Yes, the devil's agent

and his co-conspiring minions

are going down, leaving town,

scaled eyes, sticky fingers,

colored hair, law degrees,

to the end grifting and grubbing.

Numb and Number

12/24/2020

By Ventilators Encumbered

They say hindsight's 2020,

yet there's blinded folk aplenty

hindered by specks (or motes,)

lust, greed, fear and sex.

Patients on their deathbeds

calling Covid-19 a hoax —

passed 3.14(100,000) deaths like a dirty shirt.

18,000,000 cases in the U.S.,

good for number 1 in the world

in the race against India, Brazil, Russia et al.

"But I don't find masks comfortable."

"Well, you really won't like a ventilator."

Short of medical workers —

short of ICU's —

short of hospital rooms —

but long on graft and pardons.

3300 deaths a day we suffer.

Bild: "Alle vier Minuten stirbt ein Deutscher."

326,000 total, and skyrocketing —

Inquiring minds will break the code, 666 —

some basketball scores: 102-96, 98-82, 79-65,

Lions 68-Christians 0.

In a number of weeks

he'll learn how many indictments

the prosecutor seeks,

and how many of his cronies will curse

his satanic, deluded, incoherent

promises and inflated/deflated numbers,

even the size of his inauguration crowd.

Numb and Number

1/19/2021

1:22 CST

Death Will Not Slumber

400,000 succumbed to death and his minions,

legions that enabled Trump, Azar,

Navarro, talk radio (a host of hosts),

and credit, too, to the Grim Reaper, Moscow Mitch,

who earlier oversaw

the quiet death of numerous bills sent over by the house.

Mitch's reign of error is ticking to an end.

Is it 4000 deaths a day?

X per minute in LA County?

Y in refrigerated morgue trucks?

Limits on the number of cremations?

(Gotta think of air pollution, you know.)

And a rising rate of hospitalizations in TN?

Arizona replaces South Dakota

as the hotspot in the world?

What about my God-given right to worship?

With hundreds of fellow believers?

And by the way —

I don't like the way the mask feels.

Note to the Covid-denying mask-refusing

Trumpers as they infect each other (and us):

you really won't like the way

a ventilator feels as you die

among strangers, denied a goodbye kiss.

Numb and Number

1/30/2021

Saw That Lumber

10:30 – 11:00

2,200,000 deaths globally, 102,000,000 cases.

One rocker, five or six benches,

a table and a straight-back chair —

driven outdoors during Covid-19

to fashion something usable from scrap.

25,000,000 cases, 436,000 deaths in our country —

700,000 cases and 9500 deaths in TN —

slow to vaccinate, quick to die —

while some equivocate and deny.

Five died as a result of an insurrection,

with two law enforcement suicides to follow.

The incessant escalation of numbers —

relentless accumulation of facts —

the process takes its toll

by dint of weight and persistence.

From 1967 watching Bonnie and Clyde

to 1972 with The Godfather,

from revulsion at the fusillade

and bullet holes in Bonnie's dress

to the casual acceptance

of the hit at the security gate,

the gradual lessening of care and concern.

It was almost like saying,

Shoot him again, he's still wiggling.

Numb and Number

2/7/2021

What's in a Number?

9:50

462,000 dead, 5,000 in one day.

What shall we say?

Is there a magical mythical mystical

element embedded in 666?

Or something divine about 7?

And some troikas proved unsatisfactory.

We can squeeze countless lessons

from 144,000, from the Book of Numbers,

and from the remaining 65.

Yet some take the global cases and deaths —

105,000,000 and 2,300,000 respectably —

(a la Dizzy Dean) as a hoax, as fake news.

I will now advise the wise

collect the numbers to analyze

torture the data

contort them

to the faithful report them

and they'll eventually

confess that truth is lies

black is white

and more is less.

Numb and Number

2/21/2021

Saul slew his 1000's,

David his 10's of 1000's;

who said we have maybe 15 cases,

they'll be gone to 0 soon ... like a miracle?

Made a note at 10,000 —

20,000 and a steady rise

and now we grieve 500,000 —

i.e. 11101000010010000 —

to flood our minds with memories

and our mental ears with the

click and clack of the adding machine.

Who said he'd drain the swamp?

Yeah, like Count Dracula drained

a nation's lifeblood

and a certain carnie-conman

picked the pockets and bank accounts

of his pitiable deplorable

suckers and losers.

Numb and Number

4/4/2022

Indicted, Donnie Lil' Dick —

arraigned as well.

Where were Shaman,

Q-Anon and Ashley?

The guy from Hartselle,

Enrique and Stewart Rhodes?

He belongs in the Outhouse

not the White House.

For now his trip to the courthouse

is expected to be one of several.

Thinking D.C., stolen classified info – –

Georgia, gimme a break fellas,

I just need X votes (with an artificial vowel in "votes",
– – -)

Swalwell's suit, E. Jean Carroll,

the list goes on.

If convictions come

can jail be far behind?

Numb and Number

5/05/2024

The U.S. passed the 1,000,000 mark in Covid-19
deaths.

As to my poem on the subject —

what else can I say?

juan n der Wildnis

CHAPTER 39

FOGGY MORNING BREAKDOWN

It wasn't just

the foggy mornings,

or the isolated

mountain cove

that drove

him to a so-called

breakdown.

Rain or shine

would have been just

as fine.

And he was more alone

in traffic than at home.

Twice a week he made the trip

to bridge an artificial gap,

to make the leap

from familial fiddle

to virtuoso's violin.

He strained his neck

to expand his repertoire

and master the next technique.

But as he progressed

more and more

he realized,

if he were to play right,

his best

bet yet

was to relax his grip

a little,

hold the bow close

to his heart

and play less with his mind.

Maybe then he could

clear his head

in the morning fog

and pull himself together

in that isolated

mountain cove.

His few neighbors think it strange,

even queer,

in remembering the drop

from such high hopes

to such a narrow sphere.

Still they stop

when passing

to get a look

should he so properly prop

against his porch post.

Some of the townspeople say

he couldn't play

by the book.

Two or three old-timers

are reminded of his grandpa

and how he loved to drink.

Yet the very folks

who crack the jokes

in passing

still stop

to try and hear,

should he rosin up

for his best friends,

the bear, the cat, the mink.

But if you ask me

he will endure.

He became a new creature

when he left his teacher.

That's why on foggy mornings

in an isolated

mountain cove

soul-stirring strains and notes

come together for those

who still stop

in high hopes

they'll get to hear,

they'll get to see,

beauty alone

once.

Sept. 30, 1989

juan n der Wildnis

CHAPTER 40

ANDREW GINGRICH'S DYING

Clip, clop, clippety clop

Up to the top

Of the poplar steps

At a nightspot called Ponderosa.

You'd think Andy's sorrel

Gelding would stop.

But Andy, being drunk with wine,

Rode him inside,

Where he did allegedly

Perpetrate the crime immoral

Of assault with intent to commit murder.

Einige verlassen sich auf Wagen und Rosse.

There's many a slip

Twixt the plow and the grip

Of a Browning semiautomatic;

And many a mile

From that Amish domicile

To a world gone haywire.

The brethren led a quiet life,

Working with their hands,

Agrarians at peace on the land.

Andy could remember

From the tender age of two

The soothing

Coo

Of a distant dove

At evening milking time.

Later, the sight, the smell, the sound

Of a pair of draft horses

Breaking new ground for his father.

Living so close to the soil he

Erred a

Bit as we all are wont to do.

More appealing to him than a rustic

Bower

Was a frosty Ponderosa brew.

His hope of glory and honor

Was replaced with an appreciation

Of power as practiced by the world.

So he deserted the pacifist preaching

And found himself reaching

For the powder of the Browning,

Which he learned to use

Without dropping a

Tear.

Die Waffen, mit denen wir kaempfen,

sind nicht schwach wie Menschenwaffen.

Perhaps it was a grudge

Or even simple spite

That drove him back that night;

He himself couldn't have said.

But caught as a stranger

In the vice of two worlds,

Trapped between two tongues,

Suffering self-inflicted guilt,

He shot up the place.

Der Geist selbst tritt fuer uns ein

Mit unaussprechlichem Seufzen.

So it was that the judge

Prepared to hear the case,

But the news broke

That Andy had been found

Down by Big Oak

Between the colony and town.

Plop, plop, sickening plop —

First the rifle, then Andy,

Then the blood, drop by drop.

My prayer, dear Andrew,

Is that the angels might make your

End a

Confirmation of all that's true,

And teach the

Rest

To lighten the load

That you were unable to

Tote.

In jenen Tagen werden die Menschen suchen,

Und nicht finden,

Den Tod.

CHAPTER 41

OLD HICKORY DECAYED

Hickory Dickory Dock

Jenny's biological clock

Has now wound down.

Slain at the compulsive hand

Of a long-term loser

More or less killing time,

She was eventually found

Barely buried in the loamy leafy land

Not far from Yellow Creek Road.

Hickory Dickory Dock

Jenny's easy to knock

Now that she can't open her mouth.

Her family has taken —

Money, votes, land, respect, power —

From the public for years

While she struggled with a load

The others couldn't understand.

While William and Jimmy played

God at Goodluck and got rich

Young Andy hid behind

The courthouse door and family fame

But didn't "need to answer your questions."

Yes, your God-forsaken

Daughter/sister brought you tears.

CHAPTER 42

WATCH OSCAR

Seven come eleven, talk to me bones, you pays your

Money and you takes your chances.

You don't have a Chinaman's chance,

Or a snowball's chance in hell.

But the God of all odds,

Who can transform dispersal into reunion

And reversal into communion,

Can surely install nerve enough in the lost soul

To set foot upon the unknown road.

Since the journey seems eternal,

Since a multitude of thoughts and doubt

From within and from without

Would extinguish that final flicker

Of hope's last candle,

Winter clouds assemble,

Scarce believing the possibilities.

The debate raged, and a few placed their bets.

The experts claimed he carried too much baggage

To reach the impossible goal.

Eyewitnesses swear they traveled light,

Hauled it all in a Chevette by night.

What nobody saw

Was the memory of what had been,

The hope of what lay ahead,

The certainty that every weakness is made perfect

In another strength.

They were two tiny streams,

One maybe two miles longer.

But after flowing together about eleven miles

They diverged at an old millstone

To meander another six miles,

Independent and unaware of each other,

Before finally converging with each other once more

On their rocky downward course.

There could be rapids and shoals ...

There could be hostile tribes ...

Or even Leviathan.

So what's the difference

In the two watery routes

If both are taken?

One is hope personified

(Except hope that is seen isn't hope,)

The other, hope delayed but not denied.

juan n der Wildnis

CHAPTER 43

THE EXECUTION OF BETTY LOU

Beelzebub and Beetlegeus

Conspired in faint light

To expedite

Betty Lou's

Lonely venture home.

Now a feast for flies

Her body lies

Mortally injected.

Texas is protected.

Meanwhile Sammy the Bull Gravano

Had been free

To buy and sell Ecstasy,

Though he had sent nineteen

To the gates of hell.

And L.A. has defrauded

Thousands through the years

Even as Gates lauded

His cronies on the force

As the finest he'd seen.

Yes, the eyes of Texas

Well up in compassion

For grandma's dead exes

While Junior the Flawless

Holds the mansion

Against the lawless

Who happen to be poor and dumb.

Should not the world have shuddered

When Daddy's ticker fluttered?

What would he have said,

The Lord of Lies,

If his dad were dead?

Would he realize

That the law of light

Will triumph over night?

CHAPTER 44

CELESTIAL FRIEND

Is your path a faulty circle

Or a recurrent ellipse?

Is there a way for you to know

Your part of an eternal duo?

Junior partner in an orchestrated eclipse?

Not exactly in the shadow,

Nor to generate either heat or light.

In spite of your lesser glory

You are always a one-faced character,

Not given to distort the light.

You transverse, faithfully and simply reflecting,

Neither adding nor subtracting a tittle.

Sail on pale nocturnal wafer.

Live out your calling, play your part

In the universal liberating story.

Let there be light,

Even in the dark of night.

CHAPTER 45

I'LL PASS

O grave, what do you bring

That concerns me at all?

O death, where is your sting?

Right in your face I will sing,

And arise even though I fall.

O grave, what do you bring?

Do you see me wring

My hands at your puny pall?

O death, where is your sting?

Let me tell you one other thing —

You can keep your haloperidol.

O grave, what do you bring?

No, to this life I will not cling,

And for you I will not crawl.

O death, where is your sting.

O, my hope is the King,

And His glory is at my call.

O grave, what do you bring?

O death, where is your sting?

CHAPTER 46

WHAT TO DO

Yeah, we know Heartbreak Hotel,

And all about the Lorraine Motel.

We have peeped through keyholes

And seen the whole world on stage.

King Cotton trumped the mud and slime.

Why, the ducks at the Peabody

Waddled to and fro

In better straits than the fans on Beale Street.

We went, we saw, we lamented.

They say a small-time thief

Slew a flawed giant here,

And a mystery-man misdirected

The cops when that king died.

Yeah, a Mississippi governor

Squired his Memphis paramour

Around this modern version

Of that ancient African town.

But what shall we do?

Cry in the Chapel?

Report the crime?

Relay the sludge?

Recount and summarize

The deaths, the thefts, the lies?

Or fling ope the door,

Confront the Babylonian whore,

And pray for the Father of Lies?

Would to God that the death knell

Of all things satanic would peal

From Graceland to the Pyramid.

Hopeless of grace

Yet we cling to the hope of grace.

We will do.

Jan. 24, 2004

juan n der Wildnis

CHAPTER 47

JAMES E.

James E.

Claims he

Was framed.

The Gandhi gunman

Had a lofty motive.

In acts purely emotive

We have shot down

The mountaintop event

And cut down the noble dreamer

Who suggested we repent.

Little men,

Having sold their souls,

Secured their spot in history.

They persecuted the prophets,

Crucified the Christ.

Even now they seek

A lowly office out of which

Any duly elected son-of-a-bitch

Can perpetrate

All kinds of misery.

CHAPTER 48

A FATHER'S VILLANELLE

So long as I draw breath and powder burns,

So long as lions roar at catching prey,

So long will I guard the heart that yearns.

If any man your vision ever spurns,

Asks how long can hope endure, simply say,

So long as I draw breath and powder burns.

Between our hope and faith an ocean churns

Our circumstances, but we're on our way.

So long will I cherish the heart that yearns.

Even when I rest beneath the moss and ferns,

Or the eagle gnaws my liver away,

So long will I cherish the heart that yearns.

More enduring than all the Grecian urns,

Longer lasting than Aten's brightest ray,

So long as I draw breath and powder burns,

So long will I guard the heart that yearns.

May 14, 1988

CHAPTER 49

FALL OF THE YEAR

What do we here, O father dear?

What do we hear?

With only each other

In the fall of the year?

Must I write her, O father, sir?

Must I write her?

Yes, I called her "Mother,"

Til the fall of the year.

Why should I leave, Dad?

Why should I leave?

I have found another

For the fall of the year.

The day is nigh, Old Man,

To say goodbye.

We will love each other

Through the fall of our years.

CHAPTER 50

HOPE UNTIL THE END

You can't go home again, my man,

You can't go home again.

The wisdom of the past is plain,

You can't go home again.

Today is made to hope, my friend,

To hope until the end.

Today's opinion tests the wind

And dares define the end.

Tomorrow brings another day,

A day to see it plain.

And then we'll surely help the man

Who stumbled on the way.

CHAPTER 51

THE DEED IS DONE

Love and need are one;

Work is play for mortal stakes.

And the deed was really done

For truth and future's sakes.

If e'er the twain should meet,

Reconciling east to west,

I say that time is best

When the deed's fragrance is sweet.

The blend of blind and sight,

Of energy, wave and light —

The deed has been done,

Making dream and deed one.

Complementarity,

That's what they'll see

Is left for the grand son.

The deed is finally done.

CHAPTER 52

RECALL HIM

Recall him whose

Aspish poison spews

And spills from the bench,

Parked for life

In a solar eclipse.

Defy him whose

Waspish pen presses

And prejudice dispossesses,

Before the spine melts,

Before the will dies,

Before the lifeblood drips.

Forget the bruise

Sustained in the fight

And the recurring relapse

Of faulty sight.

Rather focus on the waters

That promise to drench

The poor souls beneath the bench,

To stream in purity through the pall,

And may wash him as well

Who claps the tolling bell.

CHAPTER 53

MATCH THE MUSIC

Match the music to the words

And the foliage to the tree.

Match the feathers to the birds,

The fishes to the sea.

Match the mountain to the sky

And the captive to the free.

Hear hello and then goodbye

Come together naturally.

Match the winter to the spring

And the puppy to the child.

Match the silver to the ring

And the timid to the wild.

Match the ending to the start

And the fragment to the whole.

Marry language to the heart

And the music to the soul.

CHAPTER 54

SHOULDER TO THE BOULDER

Dost thou need a weather-check?

Or public opinion poll?

Why canst thou not

Put a feeble shoulder

'Gainst the whelming boulder?

Canst thou life choose

When faced with death?

What do you have to lose?

While you still have breath

Lay hold of the

Rock and roll

The Barrier away.

To the lost shout,

"Come forth!"

That mercy might

Triumph over judgment.

ONE SERVING THREE

In the beginning Love.

Then feet of clay,

And grass that withers

From time to time.

But in the give and take,

In the racket, in the rush,

No matter how you slice it,

Service makes you or breaks you.

juan n der Wildnis

A RUFF LANDING

AKA Playing Peoria

Make war the star of the show,

Wed the tech to the dough.

Graft the power to those of the right,

Who do the voodoo chant

And get the born-again

corn-again patter down pat.

Call the North star a sign

Of contraband justice,

And label books of acid aides

A fatal case of staff infection.

Appoint the looters and reelers

liars and dealers

lawyers and sundry stealers.

Prod the poor with pickles,

Ply them with ketchup,

And perhaps a pinch of bootstrap.

The zodiac maniac

Waves his rabbit's foot on the tarmac,

Cups his ear and turns his back,

Just like das Beste aus Reader's Digest.

May 6, 1988

CHAPTER 57

5TH AVENUE

Waltz with me down Primrose Lane,

Near the Avenue (5th Avenue)

And admire the stately old oaks.

Fondly recall their nicknames

Whilst we try and check

Our beagles in their pursuit of a golden calf.

Here a sapling in its tender years,

There a gray-barked grasshopper lodge.

See them tremble on the bough? Mere bait

For every Tom, Dick and Harry Fisherman

That plays Sargent one weekend a month.

Some winners, others losers.

Some trees winners, others losers.

Some for hay barns, others for gay dens.

Even one old hickory to remind us

Of our golden rule days.

Whose wood this is no one knows —

Home as often to Wild Turkey

As to mimus polyglottos;

As cozy to the polecat

As to the buzzard.

Likewise, a refuge for the snake and the maggot.

Yes, Virginia, a sterling grove withal,

Risen from an erstwhile gaggle of blue-blooded nuts.

CHAPTER 58

EAGLE-EPTIC

Many many years ago

In the Oliverian age

Dwelt an eagle hetman sage

'bove the sparrows down below.

Perched upon his eyrie grand

With his mate and young to side,

Free to fly and safely glide,

Hetman ruled that noble land.

Now the sparrows on the plain

Led a lovely life of ease,

Flitting, darting 'mongst the trees,

Not concerned with earthly gain.

Learned hetman passed a law.

Every sparrow had to pay —

Seven bugs, a twig of hay,

Forty feathers and some straw.

While collecting tax one day

Hetman overheard a threat;

"This will drive our national debt

Through the ceiling if we pay."

White was Hetman's face with rage

Learning sparrows dare oppose

Legal taxes. So he rose

To his eyrie war to wage.

Sparrows are by far too small

To engage their larger foe.

So before the cock did crow —

Feathered backs against the wall.

Hetman put them in a queue,

Laying down the law and more.

Then he stomped and snarled and swore.

When he finished, bugs were due.

"Noted aquiline on high,"

Interjected Burger Craw,

"We were listening to your law.

Give us time to scour the sky."

An extension time was set,

And without a moment's rest

Sparrows sadly launched their quest,

Hetman booming, "Don't forget!"

Now the story would be through.

But when Burger Craw returned,

He found his eyrie burned.

He decided what he'd do.

So extraordinary was

This impending threat that all

Sparrows far and wide were called.

Each was glad to serve the cause.

Older sparrows favored draft.

Younger kinfolk said to wait.

Wise ones said negotiate.

Came a voice from passing raft:

"I detect a spirit here,

One of fevered martial lust.

Sparrows, I submit you must

Raise yourselves above this fear."

"To protect our interests here,"

Came the rash and rude reply,

"We will fight and we will die.

Never shall we shed a tear,"

"Plain to see you're not afraid,"

Came response from raft afloat.

"What about your blinding mote?

Anyone among you prayed?

Who's to hurl the 'nitial stone?

Who will turn the other cheek?

Is there one among you meek,

Who can call this world his own?"

"Fool!" went up the shout and cry

From a thousand sparrow lungs.

And a thousand narrow tongues

Sentenced peaceful lout to die.

So in time the feathers flew.

So did blood and guts and eyes.

Hetman's through with greed and lies.

Hetman finally got his due.

Who's to say who won the fight?

Sparrows many? Hetman dead?

Is there anything unsaid?

When will fighters see the light?

juan n der Wildnis

CHAPTER 59

ONE PERSPECTIVE
ON THE LAW

In defense of compromise

Let's dispense with truth and lies

Dealing only with reality,

Summum bonum, practicality.

Proposition number one,

After all is said and done —

Keep on rolling with the flow, my friend.

Who will know the diff'rence in the end?

And assumption number two,

Taking all the credit due,

Changes never start with noble fools.

Only men with money make the rules.

Corollary number three:

What's good for you and me

Is only admiration for the strong

And forgetting there's a right and wrong.

Fourth, the law for modern man:

Situation ethics can

Make you happy when you're blue.

Let me tell you what you gotta do.

Just recite the Constitution,

They'll inject you with solutions.

Or invoke the Holy Bible —

They'll label that as libel.

Bow before the party system,

Tell your friends you really missed'em.

Free yourself of all restrictions,

Rise above all convictions.

Mary, Mary, quite contrary,

Inconsistent, arbitrary.

Memorize these rules, and honey,

Twist'em round and make some money.

Now the fifth commandment's neat.

It describes how men compete,

And declares how promotions can be got

If you kiss a certain well-known spot.

You'll agree that number six

Is among the slicker tricks.

It's the rule of thumb that judges use

In deciding which of these to choose.

juan n der Wildnis

CHAPTER 60

FIRE ON FIRE

AKA Basic Training

Come here shitbird! Run in place!

Attention! About face!

Scale higher and higher walls.

Speak up like you've got a pair of balls!

Stand up straight! Show some class!

Start to think and your ass is grass.

Feint and parry, bob and weave,

Keep a trump up your sleeve.

The best defense

Is a good offense.

If ninety percent of tactics is mental

The other half might be sentimental.

In the end forget the ice.

Glory unto glory sounds nice

Tho the price is ever higher

And we always fight the liar.

Test on test, trial on trial —

Thus far we've declined that damned denial.

CHAPTER 61

NECESSITY

Time was

One ingredient in the cook's concoction,

Unmeasured,

One factor in the layer's lay,

Measured,

One essential in that marvelous

Metamorphosis.

Time is

The stuff of love

Most treasured,

The sterner part of pain

Than pain,

The magic house

Our thoughts live in.

Time will

Prove the power

Of every conviction,

Test and try us

One

By

One

(Upon Nate's beginning college, 1990)

CHAPTER 62

A SAGA: JUDGE LANIER

Come my children, you shall hear

Of the midnight flight of Judge Lanier.

All the Federales claim

They're gonna treat him just the same.

Comes the plaintiff and would pray

That his children come to stay

With their natural father, sir.

But now I see the judge wink at her.

She acts like he's her creditor.

Comes the judge in chamber suite

With the mother at his feet.

Is it any wonder then

He always rules against the men,

And pins defendants to the wall.

He removed and stripped from me

Care, control and custody

Of the children I hold dear.

If I should chance to see Lanier

I would enucleate his balls.

I promised I would tell

How Lanier left his lonely cell.

The appellate court freed

The judge because the panel agreed

A different statute should apply.

Out on bail and back at home,

Judge Lanier once more was free to roam.

Our esteemed but guilty judge

Decided still again to fudge,

And failed to meet a hearing date.

Dyer County, Tennessee —

In his mind concocted enmity

From "officials" and the like

Persuaded him to take a hike.

(He who liked the slogan, "Let'em fry!)

Calling home and sending mail,

He imagined he had left no trail.

But the agents were no fools,

They used sophisticated tools

And nabbed the balmy reprobate.

What to make of such a tale,

When it's plain to see that people fail

Every day in every way.

For starters we could simply say,

"To hell with judges, one and all."

Injudicious enchilada

Ensconced in ease in Ensenada.

Did you try the agua?

Or a hot chihuahua?

In your leisure did you bother

To reflect upon that father

You drove into despair?

If you had it all to do again

Would you be more fair,

Heed the interceding man?

Would you recommend a new

Trial for the fathers who

Lost their children in your court?

For those who meekly cowered

As the DA's brother towered,

Sneered and raised their child support.

Out of simple curiosity

Regarding your philosophy —

Would you bid your legal view

A resounding curt adieu?

Or snarl between the bars,

To the bitter end an arse?

CHAPTER 63

THAT'LL BE THE DAY

Would you like to see the day

When dragons die

And poets proudly ply

Appreciated art?

When mountains move into the sea?

The lambkin lies before the Tiger's eyes?

The waters part?

Do you long to see the time

When dead men rise?

When sight is willed the blind?

When the candle never dies?

Do you yearn to see his face,

Even as he sees your own?

To be completely known,

Embraced in perfect grace?

Is your heart's desire

To fan the fire

That burns the chaff away,

And gladly yield

A body sealed

For redemption on that day?

"Ich selbst will deinen Gegnern entgegentreten und deinen Soehnen helfen."

"Bring her meine Soehne von ferne und meine Toechter vom Ende der Erde."

"Ehe denn es aufgeht, lasse ich es euch hoeren."

Mar. 3, 1992

CHAPTER 64

FEW KNEW YOU

How could you turn your back

On the big house of a legal stepfather,

The best school system in the state,

Trips to Florida and a major-league Game?

Who knew you?

juan n der Wildnis

CHAPTER 65

POUND AT THE DOOR

Someone's pounding at the door,

From far beyond the brine

With mumbled incoherent cantos

Concerning inconsequential charges

In the only art he knows.

Struggling, from the sound of it,

To order thoughts and flesh them out;

Groping with intent to fondly

Paste a picture

Into his listener's heart.

May 13, 1986

CHAPTER 66

A NOD TO PENSKE

I guess it's out of fashion

to talk of Lott and Daschle

and call it poetry.

But tonight on channel eight

Penske read a poem with straight

face and surprised me.

You see, he took my very words

from recent nascent works,

down to invoking God's will,

which I mentioned just today

to Norma in trying to say

all the hounds on Capitol Hill

who pursued impeachment

with bloviating preachment

seem one and all to have eaten dill.

Feb. 16, 1999

REFLECTIONS OF POP

Heaven forbid

That the current reality

Mirror yesterday.

Pain or pleasure,

We drink to truth

And incremental

Differential

Growth of youth.

Jan. 23, 1988

JOY AT LAST

Winter must be settling in —

First the leafy sweater, then

The white coat again.

He doesn't come to soon

Or stay too long, tho.

That crisp halo

Around the moon

Tells me it's time to go.

He has his place

And I have mine.

Now and then orbits intertwine —

Cause enough to celebrate.

Dec. 12, 1987

juan n der Wildnis

CHAPTER 69

ANOTHER NOTE FROM UNDERGROUND

Take it from a basket case,

As it were,

Who saw in Uncle Johnny himself

With sagging jaw, clasped hands,

And crossed legs,

Blankly occupying space

Beside the casket base.

To him another sister gone,

To me an undelivered bike.

That was her.

Butcher, shopper, canner, pressing on;

Milking profits from expanding lands,

Hatching eggs

To sell the peddler for flour and the like.

Before they lay me on that cryptic shelf

Crowded now by so many

Let me say —

Her steak sandwiches were as good as any

And her smile more sincere,

Yes, more gay,

Than the smile of any sitting here.

Dec. 3, 1987

CHAPTER 70

REMEMBER KARLA FAY

There is no machismo

In the bush nor in the hills

When they push to cure the ills

Of Texas

By dispensing lethal

Injections.

Let's boil some oil

For tomorrow's Karla Fay.

Not to borrow from the Way —

Perfection's

Overcoming legal

Objections.

Some folks sat in church admiring God,

Wishing Bush would form a firing squad.

Others thought the Lord would much prefer

Death by rape and then dismember her.

CHAPTER 71

BUBBA AND ME

Bubba went to school

Left me gazing at the dancing dust

And the curling wisps

Of curvilinearity

In the sunbeams by the wood stove.

After that he entered Central High

Left me playing basketball

With youthful friends

Though my heart could hardly wait

To matriculate

And attend with him again.

On my first job

I learned how man is bent

Out of shape beneath

The wheel of someone else's fortune,

How the bruising belts and tearing teeth

And shrill whistle and unrelenting

Roar rob

One of individuality.

When I married I meant

Good, not evil.

Unity appealed,

Loneliness appalled,

Challenges appeared,

Marriage tears apart.

Is nothing forever,

Except the need to repent?

Looking back

Everywhere I went

Unfulfillment

Disappointment

Stared me in the face.

Surely this Angst

Foreshadows that

Divinest discontent.

                    Jan. 1992

CHAPTER 72

THE PHRASE OF POLLY

What language shall I borrow,

Where can I find the right sound?

Dare I depict the sorrow,

The Angst that knows no bound?

I know! The phrase of Polly,

Uddered with an arrogant twitch

Upon graduation in Raleigh:

"Lassie was a bitch!"

Americans substituted "life"

And couched it in a different tense.

Either way, the phrase is rife

With verity and sense.

Both are botched, gone in the teeth,

Beyond all hope, beyond all help,

Needing only a prayer and a wreath

As a sign that neither can whelp.

March 16, 1988

CHAPTER 73

STILL LIFE

At first glance

Quintessential existential

Images,

The abandoned wagon

Overshadows the long neglected homeplace,

Receding itself into the ever dimmer

Distance.

Empty wagon excepting aged baskets —

Tongue hanging out,

All ready to run in circles

If at all;

Wood tainted and tinted by time,

Barely surviving into the fall

Of a hazy memory.

Still, apple-picking time

Is a paean to life,

Where the harvest of fruit

Is beyond dispute.

Aug. 21, 1989

AT THAT TIME

Now I ought

To have recorded

How I thought

At the time.

Once or twice

I could afford it

But I felt

Not quite sublime.

Jewels, gems.

Insightful notions

Disappeared

On the rocks.

Mem'ry mine

Symmetric remnant

Overflow the box

Of my mind.

Feb. 1988

AT LEAST THREE

With singed brow and pock-marked face

Dooby-dooby-doo

Dubby-dubby-two

Testify to us in your native tongue

Of the trials of time

And of the time of trials —

Even of Crosses in that distant place.

Sing if you will from the saucepan

Dooby-dooby-doo

Dubby-dubby-two

That fed the fleeing wife

Serving art with cay.

Plant the original Vaty in our mind.

Sing 900 days if you can.

So, happy new year, Joe

Nineteen-eighty-eight

Nineteen-eighty-eight

Let's pray for peace in all the world

Turn the other cheek in time of war,

And convert us two into three.

Say "hi" if you see him first to Leo.

Dec. 5, 1987

CHAPTER 76

BELLE MEADE ANTS

There lived in Belle Meade two ants

That wanted to visit France.

But as they neared I-440

Phillip said to Shorty,

"My legs are killing me."

So, Shorty quite willingly

Canceled their travel plans.

Now these same two piss-ants

Wanted to meet Miss France.

So, they hired a real dandy,

A professor from Vandy

To teach them to converse.

It went from bad to worse.

They sent an e-mail

To a Parisian female

On the wines of vichyssoise

And how their ant-uncle in Boise

Was king of the hill.

One letter and she had her fill —

She angrily decreed

The ants in Belle Meade

Could go to hell.

Signed: Mademoisselle

Apr. 1999

CHAPTER 77

LO, THE MORN

All the clippings could have been hay —

Melanoma taking root in my neck —

Spores by the million in the agitated pollen —

How many years of this remain for me —

Should finish this section in thirty minutes —

A sprinkle threatens my schedule —

And the question fleetingly lingers:

If it rains on the just and on the unjust,

And yet all things are possible,

Could the rain skip my yard'n

Gently soak my garden?

April 29, 1999

juan n der Wildnis

CHAPTER 78

NO TAX LOOPER

Looper ... Looper ... I think I know the name

From somewhere back in time.

Looper ... no, that guy was Cooper,

The one who ran for the senate.

Looper ... didn't he teach at Tech?

That must have been Professor Hooper.

But still and all the same

There's a certain sadness in it,

Something more than rhyme.

If I could only recollect ...

Was it in the news?

Did we go to school together?

A lady friend? Did I forget her?

Where's my memory? Where's my muse?

Isn't he the politician

Up in Putnam County Tennessee?

Who won the grand old party's nomination?

Who was sued for abusing his power?

Sued as well for an impregnation?

You'd think a girl in her condition

Would be angling for a shower.

Now the patriarchal old-timers

Praise a prez with Alzheimer's

And pronounce Looper "off the rocker, mentally."

They say he shot a man,

His opponent, in broad daylight,

With a witness close at hand.

His victim was a firm proponent

Of victims' rights.

So, it looks like Byron Looper

Is a goner,

To be compared with Boner.

That Puerto Rican law degree

Will be to no avail —

Now he graces the county jail.

It's not for me to criticize

Nor even theorize —

Will the Log Cabin guys

Leave their candidate's behind?

It's a great democracy

Where the sin of hypocrisy

Makes the voter blind.

Are we all then finally agreed

That the courthouse,

White House and outhouse

Jointly and severally need

A super duper Looper scooper?

Nov. 1998

231

juan n der Wildnis

CHAPTER 79

ELECTION '98

Ain't it great!!

Take a man like Hooker (PLEASE),

Whose blood could hardly freeze

Though a richer shade of blue.

He garnered thirty-one percent

Against a governor who

Couldn't say exactly what he meant.

Among the politicking jerks

Was one who slaughtered Tommy Burks.

The killer longed to elevate

Himself and couldn't wait.

The victim couldn't separate

The roles of church and state.

Does it boggle anybody's mind

That fifteen hundred bought the party line?

With Looper in the cell,

And likely on his way to hell,

Did they think the man could legislate?

Or did they simply vegetate

In the polling booth,

Being blinded to the truth?

Moving on to Minnesota,

Where they had a chance to vote a

Hypocrat, 'publican, or

Independent in

As their next governor —

None expected the wrestler to win,

But win Ventura did,

And gave the lie to the myth

That we need an aristocracy

To shape our public policy.

Veer east to New York City,

Where a man of little bitty

Mental and ethical capacity

Played so loose with veracity

That his nickname of "Senator Pothole"

Was changed to "Punitive Asshole."

Down the coast a few miles

Where "Senator No" rarely smiles

We find incivility

Exceeded by instability.

The guy whose arteries are hard

And said "... better bring a bodyguard"

Wasn't in this year's race,

But tried to make the case

For his extremist friend to keep his job.

All the while Big Tobacco continues to rob

Folks around the world of health

And even life itself.

Free yourself of paralysis;

Do some simple analysis.

Commit yourself to the daunting

Task of evaluation.

You may find both parties wanting

And conclude that participation

In the process lessens

Your chance of learning lessons

About love and hate.

1998

CHAPTER 80

GURULE: PART ONE

One of the Gurules

Escaped into the toolies.

The law had planned to execute;

Now they get to shoot.

Which leads us to Bernoulli's

Principle on speed.

I guess Gurule's need

For a lessening of pressure

Made him rush to fresher

Air than the warden decreed.

My tale can't go on.

I'll have to postpone

The rest of my story,

Which may turn gory.

But for now, Gurule's gone.

Dec. 2, 1998

CHAPTER 81

GURULE: PART TWO

Into the thickets and brush

Gurule made his headlong rush,

And took his final breath

Trying to outrun death.

At least he cheated Bush.

Who'd a thought the Rangers

Would be concerned with dangers

Posed by a guy on death row?

I guess it goes to show

Truth and fiction aren't strangers.

The governor might have gloated

(Some would say "showboated")

Except Gurule headed for infinity

On the waves of the Trinity

Before they found his body bloated.

I've got a real strong hunch

Texas ethics are out to lunch.

While the law-and-order crowd

Sat in church, heads bowed,

The river beat them to the punch.

Dec. 5, 1998

CHAPTER 82

A BIRD'S-EYE VIEW

For years both hawks and doves

Concealed illicit loves

And chased that little chick-a-dee.

The buzzards in the press

Refused to second guess

The gaggle of anatidae.

Duckin', feignin', bobbin',

Slickly they were robbin'

The nation blind with their postage schemes.

They also kited checks

And then discovered sex ...

And still the party's bunting streams.

The dodos in the House

Began to rail and grouse

Because of Bill's alleged lark.

They voted to impeach

But seemed to overreach —

Imagined us as in the dark.

The boobies, coots and loons

All sang familiar tunes

That scarce disguise their pecker lies.

They parrot, crow and mock

And pander to the flock

That sucks on sap and catches flies.

Yeah, the turkeys thought we'd swallow

All their tripe and blindly follow.

Oh, they sniped and fell in tern;

Then complained that Chenoweth shouldn't burn.

Now they sniffle, sob and quail.

Their accusations, doomed to fail,

Became to them an albatross

242

And brought the bird-brains loss.

They appeared by half too clever.

Methinks they should have never

Embarked upon such foul endeavor.

With all their huffin' puffin

Rigmarole the legal eagles

Love the game of roughin'

Up opponents in this town

And try to bring deponents down,

Leaving bits of flesh for seagulls.

This group of marginal men

Discussed a cardinal sin

Only to discuss

Theres many'a former lover

With the morals of a plover,

Ready to reveal the solons lied

To us about the sin of pride.

(Start with waddling Henry Hyde.)

Now the Senate mulls

The sort of Christmas all the gulls

Who pose for Hustler can expect

If they give up being circumspect

And sing like a canary

In the D.C. aviary.

They can out another Livingston

And hear him sing, a wounded swan.

I guess by now we've heard

Enough about his lovebird,

All the leering jokes about the stork

From fans of Robert Bork

Who love to pop the cork

Amid the gropes and cackles

Of rocs and senile grackles.

For a time DeLay seemed adept;

On the elm the creeper crept;

The hearts of Hatch and Paula leapt;

The birds of prey prepped;

To the podium the speaker schlepped;

With whores the men in Congress slept;

To the mound Roger Clemens stepped;

And the phoebes wept.

CHAPTER 83

RECOLLECTION OF A SON'S AFFECTION

In my recliner

I sit and reminisce

And realize that this

Recollection

Of a son's affection —

A mental image glowingly

And yet unknowingly

Groping for paper —

May not be poetry.

So try, definer —

Whether judge, attorney, raper,

Teacher, farmer, draper.

Purse your lips and parse

Meaning, feet and meter.

You are a pesky skeeter

On a draft horse,

Which can easily flail

You with his tail.

Will you talk of truth

Or the fact that Ruth

Was home run king?

Will you speak of English law,

Inquire about my paw

And flash your diamond ring?

Carp if you will

At him who takes a stab

At beauty and truth,

And praise the gutless scab

Whose dutiful youth

Insured his intact bones

Would find their designated plot

Among agonizing groans,

And whose later years

Were spent soliciting cheers —

And all he got

Was a cheap thrill.

Mar. 1999

juan n der Wildnis

CHAPTER 84

THAT MAD LEPER

If the love of money

Is the root of ev'ry evil

You won't find it funny

If I interview the devil.

"Tell me, for example,

How you explain the hunger

Here when there are ample

Stocks and stores and stuff among us?"

The devil: "Let's refer to the scripture:

First the number's overstated.

Second, even with your

Lib'ral view of dissipated

People's rights and habits

Surely you respect the warning:

Multiply like rabbits,

And you'll work from early morning."

"Do you ever question

If our national way of living

Really is the best one?

Should we focus more on giving?"

"So, you're now contending

Giving is the greater blessing.

But I think you're bending

Rules of logic for a lesson.

Eleeomosynary

Tax-exempted enterprises

Can explain how rarely

They get cash from lower classes.

Generous contributions

From the hands of U.S. business

Swell our institutions,

Though the poor are always with us."

"Tell me, Satan, how then

do you reconcile the scripture,

' ... Cattle on a thousand

Hills ...' and others like it with your

Pride in those possessions

That belonged to some poor widow?

Do you own the treasures

Of the promised ken and wisdom?"

"Go with me to yonder

Mountaintop and see how splendid

My world is. My bond and

Oath survive though life be ended."

"Get behind me, devil;

I bet my bottom dollar

You're not on the level.

Where I'm going you're not allowed to follow."

I wasn't brought up

To get all caught up

In the abundance

Of worldly possessions.

When it came to things

Like gold and fancy rings

I found redundance

Led to depression.

As I grew older

This old boulder

Kept hurtling through space

In a frantic effort

Away from all things human,

Including business acumen.

It's like a giant race

Where a mad leper

Seeks to overtake and taint

Anyone who can't

Commit to the sliver

Of truth in his heart.

Let me stand my ground

Though all around,

Thirty pieces of silver

Rip a man apart.

                    Mar. 25, 1999

juan n der Wildnis

CHAPTER 85

NASHVILLE BANTER

The other night

A friend of mine

Was telling me a tale.

Between the wine

and candlelight

He made it sound so real.

He softly told

Of lies and pain

He'd read about somewhere,

Of love gone cold,

The ball and chain,

And headed for nowhere.

"The good ole days

Are back a ways —

I guess they're gone for good.

But now and then

Remember when

We loved them like we should."

With trembling lip

And misty eye

He gazed into his glass.

"Supposin' I

Take one more sip —

You think the pain will pass?"

As much as I

despise a lie

I told a tall tale, too.

I said, "My friend,

The pain will end.

This much I promise you."

I failed to say

How soon the day —

For me it's been ten years.

This achin' heart

Still breaks apart —

Oh, memories and tears.

CHAPTER 86

SON OF MINE

What have we done, son of mine, son of mine?

We have left the life of law,

The better life to find.

That's what we've done, O son of mine.

What have we done, son of mine, son of mine?

We have lived the law of love;

Didn't mean to be unkind.

That's what we've done, O son of mine.

What have we done, son of mine, son of mine?

We loved each other more than life;

Mine was yours and yours was mine.

That's what we've done, O son of mine.

What will we do, son of mine, son of mine,

When only one is left of the two?

We'll see the pure in heart live on —

That's what we'll do, O son of mine.

1988

CHAPTER 87

ALL-CONSUMING HOPE

I thought it through

And through it all,

My all was not enough.

At first I thought

A thought would do,

But then discovered love.

If love be gone

(Though thought be true,)

The nightingale has flown

From human view

To hidden height

To suffer endless night.

If love be not

My fondest goal,

My all-consuming hope,

The flowers fade,

The grasses wilt,

And poems die a'vine.

But love endures,

And heals the heart —

Wherein my hope is hid.

CHAPTER 88

HOW TO LIVE

How

      should

          we

              then

                 live?

              When is then? Anything but

          now.

        Why

    did I

so live?

When is "did?" Life as a kid?

                How

          Shall

       We

     Now

Live?

Now?!

Like, man, wow!

As in "today?"

"Today is the day ...."

How? We know the way.

Now? As in "hour?"

"Believe me, the hour cometh, and now is ...."

265

Quietly, at peace, by faith,
Living to love, loving to give,
Forgetting what lies behind ....
We know with His own mind
How we shall now live.

Jan. 2, 1989

CHAPTER 89

SAY-HEY KIDS

Say-hey, say-hey!

All games and fun

Back about '51.

Taboos gone,

Gemstones of new hues shone

On the diamond.

May Day! May Day!

The fun and games

Now levee claims

On the two of them.

The news shone

Through tears and fears

And seared my soul.

See the brow, the eyes,

And you'll recognize

My blood in her.

Jan. 1992

CHAPTER 90

HE CAME UP FIGHTING

Old Charon plied that river more than once —

Caesar crossed the Rubicon —

The Hollmans sailed the Atlantic —

Mildred Luton caught the spirit of a German swordsman —

How he tried to scale a wall

(The wall of shame we call it now)

In crossing no man's land

To simply see his sister.

Now Oscar floats in the Rio Grande,

His angel Angie bloated,

Lifeless arm around her Dad.

What's done is done —

But I can tell no one.

I'll simply ask that you consider:

Do you have a precious pearl,

Like a little boy, a little girl,

For whom you'd gladly

Jump into that river?

Who has told you

We'll go down together?

Who lived the dream

And came up fighting?

2019

CHAPTER 91

CAMILLE AND THE BIG "C"

If I can go

Instead of you,

I think you know

That's what I'll do.

But if the day

Should ever come

You go away

Denying some

Our fondest dream

You'll also know

His love doth seem

So apropos.

I'll never raise

A question mark —

Your earthly days

Erased my dark.

Dec. 20, 1997
Written one day after cancer diagnosis for sister-
in-law.
To be read as if by her husband, or to fit the
reader's emotion.

CHAPTER 92

NATE'S ENGLISH TRIP

You don't really need

Me to say more than God-speed

And a heartfelt bon voyage.

So, we'll sally forth

To the Metro airport,

And I'll straightway bring back

Your Japanese Cadillac

To its Taggart Avenue garage.

Nov. 1, 1997

Author's note: a bit of light rhyme written on the
roadside

of Taggart Avenue before I picked Nate up for his
England trip.

CHAPTER 93

LOOK AROUND

And what can you see?

Distorted façade

Fraction of life

Milky mirage.

Who would walk by sight?

The usual stream

Of human events

Points to might

As the supreme

Judge of man's intents.

But stopping to dream

Then looking around

Raises a frown,

Erases the doubt.

Give me solid ground.

Dec. 12, 1987

CHAPTER 94

FOR THE INMATES

Brothers, bars are not our bosses,

Simply symbols of our losses.

Kindred spirits, you and I,

Holding on until we die.

Isolated we are losers,

Jailed with rapists, thieves, abusers.

But together we can win.

Keep the faith, resist and then

Laws will crumble, barriers fall,

Justice reign, with peace for all.

Yes, your children will admire you

Even though your boss might fire you.

For a change in status quo

Is a threat to those in power.

That's a fact the lawyers know,

But refuse to honor our

Simple plea to have our kids,

Recognize their father's role.

Is there something we all did?

Other than to plug that hole?

By example and by letter

We will fight 'til things are better,

Using peace and force of truth

'Til you see again the youth

There beyond the prison walls.

There! You hear it? Freedom calls!

Brother, reach a helping hand

To your neighbor, suffering man,

That together we may see

Freedom, justice, dignity,

Like the Lord Himself intended.

Soon the "Law de greed" is ended.

juan n der Wildnis

CHAPTER 95

GUARD THE HEART

Set the heart above the mind

As the manna covered dearth,

If the father you would find.

Struggling in a daily grind?

Searching for a lasting worth?

Set the heart above the mind.

Leave the empty life behind.

Look instead for more than mirth,

If the father you would find.

Tho your name be much maligned,

Damned, renounced and cursed on earth,

Set the heart above the mind.

You'll dissolve the ties that bind,

Even win the war on girth,

If the father you would find.

Deep and dark, these two entwined,

Giving death or second birth.

Set the heart above the mind,

If the father you would find.

CHAPTER 96

FATHERS' ADDRESS

Three score and eight months ago we fathers brought forth to this arena a new commitment conceived in desperation and dedicated to the proposition that all tyranny is fair game.

Now we are engaged in a great uncivil struggle, testing whether that commitment or any commitment so conceived and so dedicated can long endure. We are writing from a distant battlefield of that struggle. We are writing to dedicate a portion of this arena as a final resting place for those fathers and sons who here gave their lives that this commitment might live. It is altogether fitting and proper that we do this.

But, in a larger sense, we cannot dedicate — we cannot consecrate — we cannot hallow this arena. The emasculated men, living and dead, who struggled here, have consecrated it far above our poor power to add or detract. The world will little note, nor long remember, what we say here, but it can never forget what they did here. It is for us the living rather, to be here dedicated to the great task remaining before us — that from these honored dead we take increased devotion to that cause for which they gave their last full measure of devotion — that we here highly resolve that these dead shall not have died in vain —that these fathers and sons, under God, shall have a new birth of freedom — and that the gates of hell shall not prevail against that freedom.

SUGGESTED READINGS

Dr. Mayer	The Country Doctor
Tim Phartain	The Trial
Barry "Moe" Lester	Operation Gray Lord
Legal Stepfathers	See Spot Run
Divorcing Moms	I Cor. 13
The Devil	The Metamorphosis
FBI	Secret Tapes of MLK, Jr.
Court of the Judiciary	Book of Job

CHAPTER 97

CHAMPS AGAIN

Some had ranked them second,

Others maybe even lower.

But the spirit beckoned

From beyond that glory shore.

First, I heard it whisper,

"Mama's calling; come on home."

Then I heard it building

On the billows, on the foam.

Louder, ever louder,

Through the season, through the year.

Now it reached the crowded

Superdome for all to hear.

Sounded like a breaker

Crashing madly 'gainst the coast;

There was no mistaking —

All could hear a growling ghost.

From the op'ning kickoff —

Yea, the tossing of the coin —

See the seconds tick off —

Who's behind the breeze a'blowin'?

Came the bold pretenders,

Talkin' trash and taught to hold.

Then the great defenders

Salted down the Sugar Bowl.

Somewhere in the distance

There's a rumble and a roar.

Sounds as though the heavens

Are at peace with Bear once more.

Jan.2, 1993-Jan.4, 1993

CHAPTER 98

SANDS OF TIME

Time, oozing and slipping,

Imperceptibly drifting.

Not like snow, though,

That has nothing to show.

More like water

In a steady drip

When you're dying for a sip

And the bottom is in sight.

Or dropping and plopping

On your face as hours

Slip by — no end in sight.

Time ... hard to get a grip on it.

Smoke, hanging heavy on a fall morn,

Or flying lightly by,

Like a cottony cloud.

November, 1988

CHAPTER 99

BLOOD AND GUTS

The bloody bug

Crushed by my truck

Uttered these luckless words:

"I'd do it again

If I had the guts."

Funny ... gut to "gut"

Converts blood to good,

Turns bug to us.

But should one put

Up much fuss

Concerning such

Unless one yearns to see

The real "gut," the G.U.T?

Sept. 30, 1988

CHAPTER 100

I AM BECOME DEATH

At rest upon completion of

A lethal weapon Sakharov

Considered politics and knew

He had to stand and swear it off.

The same for Oppenheimer, too,

As well as other engineers

Around the world consumed with fears

And labeled holocaustic seers.

But once the pigs approach the trough

And swill the scientific slop,

The sands of time and hands of slime

Insure the reaper of a crop.

Above the white of Flanders field

The workers bend at harvest time,

Attempting quick to pick the yield

Before the clouds begin to climb.
Sept. 30, 1988

CHAPTER 101

TO BOO OR NOT TO BOO

To boo or not to boo,

Por favor répondez vous.

To cheer or not to cheer,

"Diese sind die Fragen hier."

Two sides to every fence,

And both often make sense.

That Nuernberg show was splendid;

Our mushroom stoutly defended.

Too many say might makes right.

What a hellacious moral plight —

Only at the end of a war

Would we know what we fought for.

"Du bist des Gottes Sohn."

On that rock is our conviction

Against any contradiction.

Eat the meat; spit out the bone.

ABOUT THE FATHER AND SON

juan n der Wildnis is the nom de plume of a father who has compiled and composed these recollections, hopes, aspirations and challenges. A native middle-Tennessean; educated at Martin College, Middle Tennessee State University and Vanderbilt University; bonded with a son in the hay and corn fields and sweaty, humid milking parlor of a dairy farm; the author harbors the hope that the reader will keep his dreams alive and strive for a brighter future.

www.ingramcontent.com/pod-product-compliance
Lightning Source LLC
Chambersburg PA
CBHW021409110726
47901CB00008B/2122